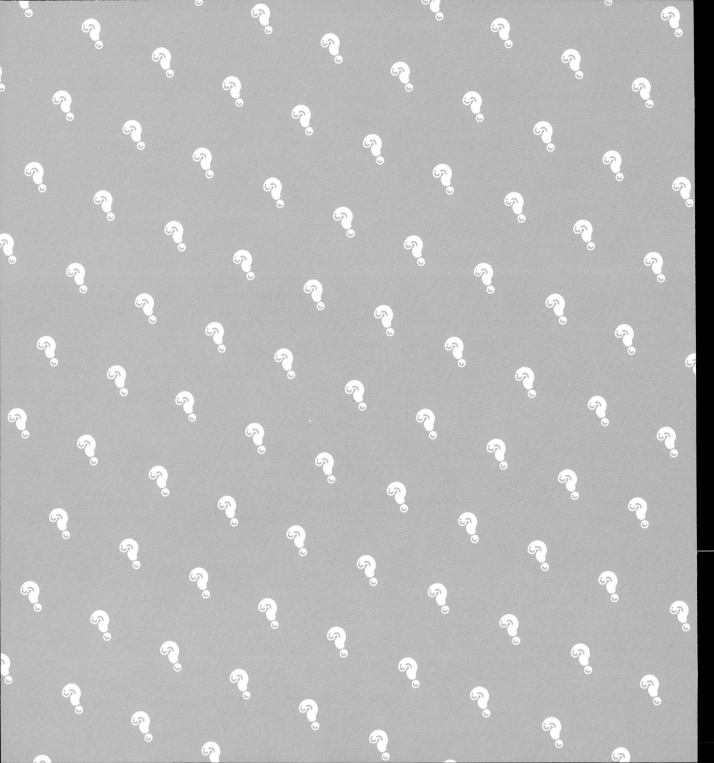

Rainboots for Breakfast

BY MARCIA LEONARD
PICTURES BY JOHN HIMMELMAN

Silver Press

For Dana and Sasha Frankel, just for fun.
—M.L.

To my brother Jim, one of my two closest friends in the world.
—J.H.

Library of Congress Cataloging-in-Publication Data

Leonard, Marcia.
    Rainboots for breakfast / by Marcia Leonard;
pictures by John Himmelman.
        p.   cm.—(What next?)
    Summary: Frog begins his day with a pleasant
breakfast. At various points in the text the reader is
asked to guess what happens next.
    [1. Frogs—Fiction.   2. Breakfasts—Fiction.
3. Literary recreations.]   I. Himmelman, John, ill.
II. Title.   III. Series: Leonard, Marcia. What next?
PZ7.L549Rai   1989
[E]—dc19   89-6016
                                                CIP
ISBN 0-671-68591-0 ISBN 0-671-68587-2 (lib. bdg.)   AC

Produced by Small Packages, Inc.
Text copyright © 1989 Small Packages, Inc.

Illustrations copyright © 1989 Small Packages, Inc.
and John Himmelman.

Published by Silver Press, a division of
Silver Burdett Press, Inc.
Simon & Schuster, Inc.
Prentice Hall Bldg., Englewood Cliffs, NJ 07632.

Printed in the United States of America.

10 9 8 7 6 5 4 3 2 1

On Saturday, Frog woke up to dark gray skies
and pounding rain. "Harrumph!" he said. "What
nasty weather. I'm going back to sleep."

Then he heard a funny noise: mumble . . .
rumble . . . grumble. It was his tummy growling!

So what do you think Frog did next?

Did he crawl under his bed to
hide from the noise?

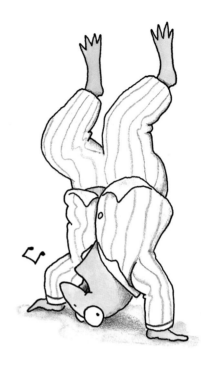

Did he stand on his head and
sing "Happy Birthday"?

Did he tickle his toes to make
himself laugh?

Or did he go downstairs to get
something to eat?

"My tummy wants breakfast," said Frog.
He put on his bathrobe and slippers and hurried
downstairs to the kitchen.

He got out a glass and some dishes, a napkin and silverware, and he set the table.

Then he searched through the cupboard and the refrigerator for something tasty to eat.

Now what do you think Frog decided to have—

a plate of dry leaves with weeds on the side,

a pair of fried rainboots with a mugful of mud,

a bowl of cereal and a glass of orange juice,

or toasted jellybeans with marshmallow fluff?

Frog ate up all his cereal and drank all his juice.
"Delicious!" he said.
Rumble . . . grumble . . . said his tummy.

"I guess I'm still hungry," said Frog. He got out a loaf of bread and a jar of strawberry jam.

He put two slices of bread in the toaster and waited until they popped up, all warm and golden brown.

Then what do you think Frog did next?

Did he spread jam on the toast and eat it?

Did he put it in the sink to see if it would float?

Did he tell it a story and tuck it into bed?

Or did he use it to wipe off the table?

Frog ate up every crumb of toast and jam. "Yum!" he said. And this time his tummy said nothing. At last it was quiet and happy.

Frog patted his mouth with his napkin. Then he got
up from the table and neatly pushed in his chair.

"First I'll put away the cereal, the juice, and the jam," thought Frog.

Then what do you think he did with his dirty dishes?

Did he sail them through the
air like flying saucers?

Did he wash them and dry
them and put them away?

Did he sweep them out the
door with a broom?

Or did he stack them in
a dark corner of the
basement?

As Frog washed his dishes, the clouds started to roll away. As he dried them and put them in the cupboard, the sun came out.

And as he got dressed, the sky turned a lovely blue.
"Hooray!" said Frog. "It's going to be a
beautiful day after all!"

Then he hurried outside to enjoy the fine weather.